A Night at the Farm

at the

Farm

A BEDTIME PARTY

C+C MINI FACTORY

RP|KIDS
PHILADELPHIA

Running Press Kids
Hachette Book Group
1290 Avenue of the Americas, New York, NY 10104
www.runningpress.com/rpkids
@RP_Kids

Printed in China

First Edition: February 2021

Published by Running Press Kids, an imprint of Perseus Books, LLC,
a subsidiary of Hachette Book Group, Inc. The Running Press Kids name
and logo is a trademark of the Hachette Book Group.

The Hachette Speakers Bureau provides a wide range of authors for
speaking events. To find out more, go to www.hachettespeakersbureau.com
or call (866) 376-6591.

The publisher is not responsible for websites (or their content) that
are not owned by the publisher.

Print book cover and interior design by Marissa Raybuck

Library of Congress Control Number: 2019950310

ISBNs: 978-0-7624-6841-6 (hardcover), 978-0-7624-6842-3 (ebook),
978-0-7624-7005-1 (ebook), 978-0-7624-7004-4 (ebook)

APS

10 9 8 7 6 5 4 3 2 1

For all the bedtime stories you told me.
abc xyz to Mama & Papa.

—Q.M.C.

For Mom and her barnyard animals:
Cow, Skunk, and Duck.

—C.C.

The orange sun sets,
the farmer stifles a yawn.
It's been quite a full day,
and she's toiled since dawn.

She's locked up the gates,
hummed her "goodnight" song.
The animals are tucked in,
but not for long . . .

The cat gives the signal
when the farmer starts to snore.
Time to jump from the bed
and sneak out the door.

The long day is over.
Now it's time for some fun.
Because when the farmer goes to sleep . . .
the party's just begun!

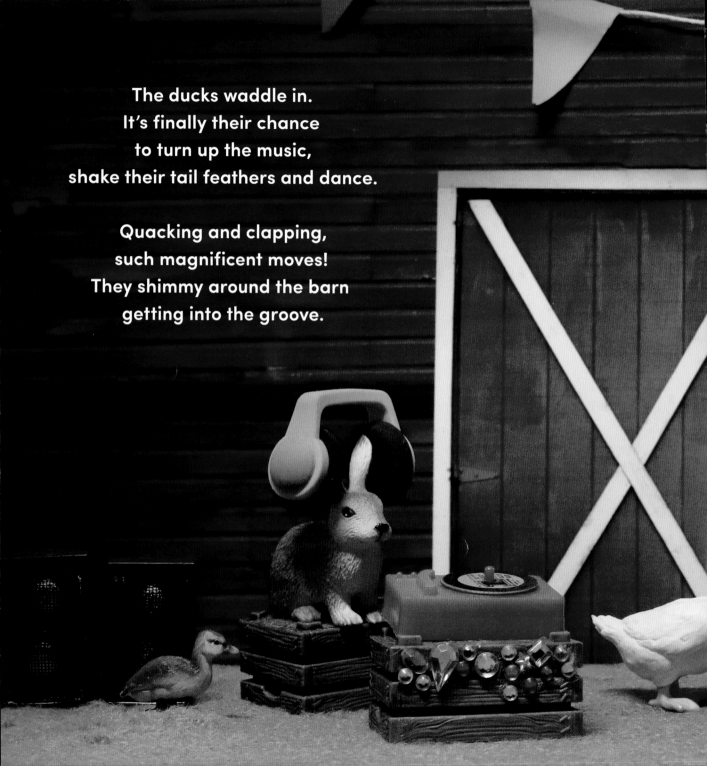

The ducks waddle in.
It's finally their chance
to turn up the music,
shake their tail feathers and dance.

Quacking and clapping,
such magnificent moves!
They shimmy around the barn
getting into the groove.

The horse tries to bake
a delicious apple crumble.
But he's got four left hooves,
so it's a bit of a fumble.

Flour, eggs, and sugar
fly through the air.
He mixes and stirs
with his own special flair.

The rabbits go out to dinner
under the night sky.
A sheep dog takes their order
as they smell . . . burnt apple pie?

They feast on, what else?
Fresh carrots and kale
so crisp and delicious,
they wiggle their tails.

Being pigs in a pen
can be the messiest job—
So they hop in the bath
they're certainly not slobs!

Hot water and bubbles!
What better way to relax
than get squeaky clean
while wearing mud masks?

The farm is ready
for the goat fashion show.
They wear fabulous frocks
and prance out in a row.

The styles are bold.
So shiny and divine!
The goats work the runway.
They're the greatest of all time.

The hen wears her cape
and invites the whole farm
to watch her perform magic
with such chicken charm.

The audience applauds.
After each trick, they gasp!
But she'll never reveal
how she cut Rooster in half.

The ducks cut a rug.
They stomp their webbed feet
and clap their wings
to the sweet, sweet beat.

It's all such a hoot
that the pigs can't resist,
and the posh herd of goats
joins in for "The Twist."

The turkey has no time
for all of that clatter.
He turns on the TV
to watch things that matter.

Super Heroes and Villians!
Fighting crime is a blast.
Turkey loves it so much,
he thinks he's part of the cast.

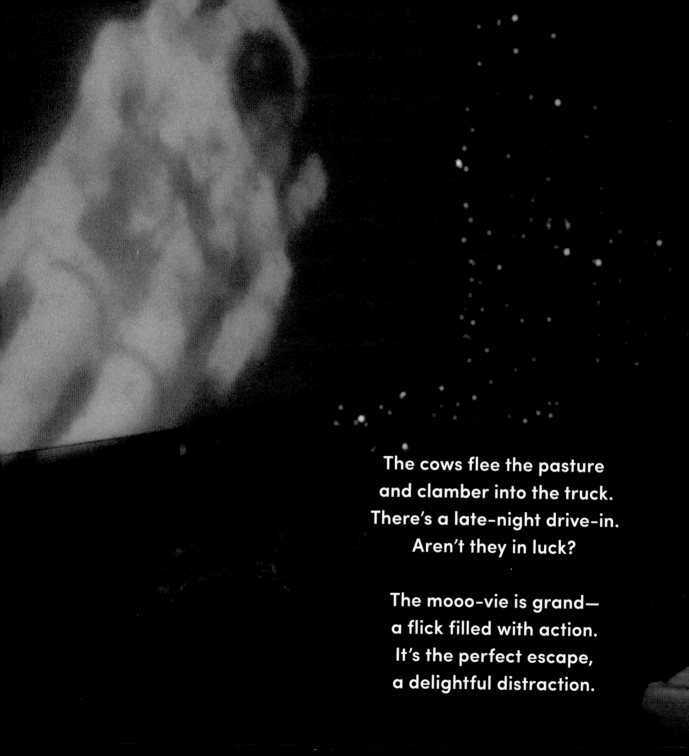

The cows flee the pasture
and clamber into the truck.
There's a late-night drive-in.
Aren't they in luck?

The mooo-vie is grand—
a flick filled with action.
It's the perfect escape,
a delightful distraction.

Back at the farm,
the dance floor is filled.
Glitter flies through the air.
The animals are thrilled!

Though the ducks dig the disco
and the pigs prefer pop,
the animals all cheer
when the beat finally drops.

The barn starts to brighten
with light from the window.
The horses slow down
and stop doing The Limbo.

The pigs are exhausted,
the sheep close their eyes.
The animals are tucked in
with content, sleepy sighs.

The rooster starts his croon
when morning has arrived.
The farmer wakes up,
feeling fresh and revived.

Over the barn,
the sun begins to creep.
And that's finally when
the farm goes to sleep.

Good night.